Tiny Treasures

FICTION FROM YORKSHIRE

First published in Great Britain in 2010 by
Young Writers, Remus House, Coltsfoot Drive,
Peterborough, PE2 9JX
Tel (01733) 890066 Fax (01733) 313524

Website: www.youngwriters.co.uk

SB ISBN 978-1-84924-939-3

Disclaimer
Young Writers has maintained every effort
to publish stories that will not cause offence.
Any stories, events or activities relating to individuals
should be read as fictional pieces and not construed
as real-life character portrayal.

Book designed by Spencer Hart & Tim Christian

Foreword

Since Young Writers was established in 1990, our aim has been to promote and encourage written creativity amongst children and young adults. By giving aspiring young authors the chance to be published, Young Writers effectively nurtures the creative talents of the next generation, allowing their confidence and writing ability to grow.

With our latest fun competition, *The Adventure Starts Here ...* , primary school children nationwide were given the tricky challenge of writing a story with a beginning, middle and an end in just fifty words.

The diverse and imaginative range of entries made the selection process a difficult but enjoyable task with stories chosen on the basis of style, expression, flair and technical skill. A fascinating glimpse into the imaginations of the future, we hope you will agree that this entertaining collection is one that will amuse and inspire the whole family.

Contents

The Mini Sagas

A Fright One Night

Frantically Ellie ran up the old creaky stairs as the thunder crashed together and the lightning flashed. Quickly Ellie hid under her pretty, pink bed when she heard loud footsteps coming up the stairs. Slowly the door opened as the figure neared her bed ... it was her grumpy sister!

Ellie Stephenson (11)

Aston Hall J&I School, Aston

The Haunted Surprise

Something was haunting me. I could feel it behind my back. The old jagged chair I was sitting in creaked. I tried to ignore it but it wouldn't go away. Then I felt something sloppy across my face. I had to look and there was my pink little dog, Susie.

Mollie Hobson (11)
Aston Hall J&I School, Aston

Home Alone

I woke up, nobody was there. I was so scared I started to sweat. The house was silent, the dog snarling. I walked downstairs, I started crying. Floorboards creaking, I opened the door ... *phew,* my mum and dad were in the garden.

'Hello darling.'

'Love you Mum and Dad.'

Jade Pugh (10)

Aston Hall J&I School, Aston

The Monster

I am going in now. Cautiously I open the wooden door and step inside. It is pitch-black, I turn my torch on and see an extremely tall, green figure made out of rotten fruit, old shoes and *snot!* I run home, I hope I will never go there again.

Katie Taylor (10)
Aston Hall J&I School, Aston

Run To Safety

Boom! Tammy heard footsteps chasing her. As she ran along the corridor the monster followed her. Suddenly the monster cried out, 'Come back!' *What? I must be dreaming,* thought Tammy as she turned round to face it. An arm reached up and took off the mask. It was her brother.

Eleanor Wilson (10)

Aston Hall J&I School, Aston

Silence

Suddenly Luke ran into the old crooked house. It
was silent and dark, the shadow of a companion
stood there licking his lips. 'Hello Cole.'
'Hello friend.'
'What are you doing here?' I said.
'Nothing, nothing.' Then the room went silent.
With a blink of an eye it was over ...

Luke Rumboll (10)
Aston Hall J&I School, Aston

Skin Deep!

One night, five girls were having another sleepover and it wasn't going so well again because they heard smashing glass and ear-shattering shrieks and thumping up the stairs! 'I'm back for more skin!' Then a piece of skin got thrown in the bedroom.
There was silence, then, *'Argh!'*

Joseph Hobson (10)
Aston Hall J&I School, Aston

Bonfire

On Bonfire Night all I could hear was *bang, bang, pop,*
sizzle, sizzle! It was very loud, I was very scared. The
trees were waving like people doing the Mexican
wave, people were screaming and laughing. I could
barely hear the music. The bonfire was spitting,
burning everywhere.

Mia Russell (10)
Aston Hall J&I School, Aston

Boo!

I stood there in the gloomy darkness, counting in my head; 'Here I come,' I called. I searched around the woods looking for her. Suddenly I heard a noise in the massive bush, 'Boo!' it said.
'It's only me,' shouted Lucy.
'Phew, I wondered who that was then,' I said.

Olivia Patchett (10)
Aston Hall J&I School, Aston

Halloween

Bang, flash, crack! What was that? I hear footsteps coming closer and closer ... I hear a knock at the door ... I open it, I see a deadly sight, a terrifying, horrific vampire. His teeth sparkle in the light.
'Argh!' I scream.
'Trick or treat?'

Tamzin Snelling (9)
Aston Hall J&I School, Aston

Wedding Ring Surprise

Slowly turning the knob I walked into the monster-shed. There, lying on the brown table, was a blue box. Shakily opening it, my boyfriend jumped out and said, 'Will you marry me?' I replied, 'Yes!' and we lived happily ever after.

Charlotte Murdoch (9)

Aston Hall J&I School, Aston

Darkness

Suddenly the crafty shadows lurk in the darkness.
I hear noises that chill my bones. The smell of
pure evil. Quickly the air goes cold. I taste the
fear that rations the happiness in my thoughts.
After that I never knew what it was.

Joshua Walker (10)
Aston Hall J&I School, Aston

Zombie Alert

Everywhere I looked was silent. Then I heard a giggle. I peered cautiously around my shoulder. Nobody was there. Suddenly I heard a groan. I screamed. I ran. Zombies came from behind the trees but then I noticed they weren't real zombies. They were my friends trying to scare me!

Emelia Daniels (11)
Aston Hall J&I School, Aston

The Forbidden Door!

Quietly, Mia approached the forbidden door. Without hesitation she opened it. Vibrant colours shone in her eyes. She stared into the room which was full of presents. Her intention was to go in, but she heard her mum's footsteps downstairs. She sprinted to her room and pretended to be asleep ...

Hannah Fitzgerald (11)
Aston Hall J&I School, Aston

The Christmas Present

Stacey stepped into the pet shop and her eyes fell on the cutest, fluffy, ginger kitten huddled in the corner of the cage. 'You can't have him,' her mother said. 'Dad doesn't allow cats in the house.'
On Christmas morning Stacey awoke and saw the tiny kitten in her stocking!

Lucy Keeton (10)
Aston Hall J&I School, Aston

The Sounds From Upstairs!

Emily heard creaking coming from upstairs. Slowly she began to walk up towards the door where the sounds were coming from. She placed the palm of her hand onto the old creaky handle and began to push the door open. Then, all of a sudden, 'Boo!' shouted her little brother!

Sarah Bushnell (10)

Fens Primary School, Hartlepool

The Farmer's Scarecrow

The old man woke up and went to the farm to do some strawberry picking. As always, he said hello to the scarecrow but the scarecrow wasn't there, he still went to pick his strawberries.
After he picked them, he walked back home and then the scarecrow appeared, dead!

Bailey Reed (10)
Fens Primary School, Hartlepool

The House Was Locked

Kelly looked scared. She turned around and realised there was a man after her, wearing all black. She started to run to her home. Suddenly the man shouted, 'Kelly, what are you doing?' She kept on running until she got home but the door was locked. So she kept running ...

Emma Carroll (10)
Fens Primary School, Hartlepool

Scary Birthday

Kevin looked suspicious as he walked through the old crooked door into the house that he'd been invited to. He walked in with terror in his eyes. It was pitch-black. The water was dripping as he walked past. *Drip! Drip!*

Now it was twelve at night. 'Happy birthday, Kevin!'

Daniel Kerridge (11)
Fens Primary School, Hartlepool

A Celebrity Holiday!

Melissa and Catherine are going on holiday. They arrive at the train station to be told their train is cancelled. A 'famous' celebrity standing nearby takes them to London in her limo. They fly to Florida with the celebrity and have a fantastic time staying at her mansion as guests.

Catherine Mason (10)
Fens Primary School, Hartlepool

The Unfortunate Escape!

The spy jumped over the high fence, hoping
he would get a head start. He sprinted to
his motorbike and rode off. Tough luck.
Unfortunately he was too slow. The master thief
had managed to climb on. The thief pulled out a
gun.
'Cut!' said the director, 'not realistic enough.'

Erin Hanson (10)
Fens Primary School, Hartlepool

An Unexpected Guest

'I don't believe in ghosts,' I said.
'You shouldn't say that, there could be one in this room,' whispered Megan, shaking so that the bed rattled frantically. Something moved under the duvet; it grabbed my and Megan's legs. Suddenly my brother's head popped out. 'Liam, you horror!'

Casey Jane Sickling (9)
Fens Primary School, Hartlepool

A Jolly Christmas

Carelessly, I ripped the present open, wondering what I could get. My mum got me a bike and my dad got me a DSi. I was over the moon. I thanked my parents. I opened the rest of my presents enthusiastically and had a very jolly Christmas with everyone.

Megan Lancaster (9)

Fens Primary School, Hartlepool

Elves' Disaster

It is Christmas Eve. An elf comes pounding up to Santa. 'We have not got Emily's present and it is Christmas Eve!'
They need to go on a hunt. They go down a horrifying chute; a slippery sliding conveyor belt. And then after that they get the presents. It's saved!

Emily Attwood (9)
Fens Primary School, Hartlepool

Terrifying Halloween

It was Halloween, Molly was terrified. Her mother said she would be home at 5pm and it was 8pm. Suddenly the living room door opened with a creak. Her mother jumped out. She shouted, 'Trick or treat?'
Molly exclaimed bravely, 'Mum!'

Chloe Moore (9)
Fens Primary School, Hartlepool

Santa Surprise

One night, after a great night out, I went home.
It was pitch-black. I was all alone, nobody was in
the house. The door opened, Santa came out and
shouted, 'Surprise!'
Cakes and presents, it was the best day of my life!
'Merry Christmas to all people!'

Jones Lawson (9)
Fens Primary School, Hartlepool

Christmas Fave

In the morning it was Christmas Eve - one day till Christmas Day. We were all excited. We waited till dinner, then all of my family came for Christmas dinner, we had a great time.
I went to get my pyjamas on and I got a great, great shock ...

Owen Baker (9)
Fens Primary School, Hartlepool

Christmas Eve

On Christmas Eve I'm so very happy, watching all
the families enjoy their lovely Christmas. We all
go shopping - I say to my mum, 'I want this.'
Then I wake up in the morning on Christmas Day,
go to look at my presents but it's not snowing.

Corey Griffiths (9)
Fens Primary School, Hartlepool

Untitled

Daniel was in the attic with his friends, telling ghost stories. They were playing pranks on Michel. 'What was that?' said Michel. 'I don't know.' There was a creak - silence. 'Ooooooo,' said a ghostly voice. 'Tea!' shouted Mum. The boys ran downstairs. Mum started laughing.

Alex Boynton (9)
Fens Primary School, Hartlepool

Rudolph's Got Flu!

On Christmas Eve Santa was loading his sleigh for
the busy night ahead. But when he checked on his
reindeer, he realised that Rudolph's red nose was
blue! 'Oh Rudolph, what's wrong?'
'I've got flu,' said Rudolph.
'Oh no, we'll have to go without you, sorry.'
'Oh man!'

Rachel Esther Blakey (9)
Fens Primary School, Hartlepool

Creepy Christmas!

It was Christmas morning. I was so excited, so I went to get my parents and went downstairs to open our presents. That's when something terrible happened. My parents disappeared! It was like, one minute they were there, and the next they weren't. Then all I heard was screaming. 'Thomas!'

Thomas Waites-Hunter (9)
Fens Primary School, Hartlepool

Mwhahaha!

Creak! 'Hello?' she said.
'Mwhahaha!' said a vampire. Bats flew, cobwebs lit up the room.
Meanwhile she saw the vampire, 'Argh!' She ran for her life.
'I'll catch you some day!' angrily shouted the vampire!

Ellis Wall (10)
Fens Primary School, Hartlepool

The Old Church

The old church bell struck twelve o'clock. Georgia and Holly knocked on the door, nobody answered. They waited a couple of minutes. They started to walk away but it creaked open slowly. They turned around, to their astonishment, there was a man standing there, dribbling and growling with hunger.

Jessica Masey (11)
Fens Primary School, Hartlepool

The Lucky Bag

Paragliding in the USA, Bill saw a rare bird. Bill got his camera out of his bag. Suddenly he lost control of his glider. He spun rapidly and came out of his harness. Bill fell to the ground, the bag caught on a branch and broke his fall.

Matthew Hughes (10)
Fens Primary School, Hartlepool

Haunted Rover

Lucy and Rover, her doggy companion, wandered inside, not knowing where to go. Suddenly *creak!* Rover scampered up the stairs. 'Rover!' Lucy went further inside to search for him. 'Oh no!' she said to herself. She went to the window.

Howl, howl!

What was that? She looked closer, 'Oh Rover!'

Heather Priestman (10)

Fens Primary School, Hartlepool

The Underwater Adventure

'Hey Harry, do you want to come with me?' said
Sam.
'Yeah,' screamed Harry.
'I'll get the sub ready,' replied Sam.
They went to Sam's house and went into the
submarine. They went into the Pachena Triangle,
then went home again.
'So, want to go in my rocket tomorrow?'

Sam Walsh (10)
Fens Primary School, Hartlepool

Screaming Flying Monkey

The men were closing in on me. They were very, very big. Then, all of a sudden, came a screaming flying monkey in a black cape and his apprentice, a screaming flying pig!

But that is a story for another time. The monkey grabbed the man and handcuffed him.

Harry Mosley (10)

Fens Primary School, Hartlepool

Untitled

'Ho, ho, ho!'
Tim ran over to Santa and gave him a big hug. 'Santa!' Tim started to run around the room, when he turned around, Santa was gone but then Santa burst through the door again. *Weird, the other Santa had a long beard. Very weird!* Tim thought. 'Santa!'

Sean Skinner (10)
Fens Primary School, Hartlepool

The Fluffy Monster!

Katie walked in the dark house. She stopped for a second, she felt a shiver down her spine. All of a sudden, something was circling her legs, it felt fluffy. She looked up, there was a light switch. She turned it on. She looked down, it was only the cat!

Emily Weatherill (10)

Fens Primary School, Hartlepool

Untitled

One day, when a rap artist called Eminem was in
his mansion, eating his favourite dinner, sausage,
mash and gravy, he heard a loud bang on his door.
He thought, *should I check?*
He got up from his chair. Eminem opened the
door and a sword stabbed him. 'Argh!'

Adam Peacock (10)
Fens Primary School, Hartlepool

The Dream

Fear contorted Tim's battered face, like an army of ants colonising new territory. The only sound was the menacing trees waving their bare arms as if trying to lure him into their deadly trap. Suddenly he awoke, light forced itself into his innocent eyes. 'Wow!' he exclaimed, 'what a dream!'

James Brooks (11)
Hutton Rudby Primary School, Hutton Rudby

Dreams Could Be Real!

Dinosaurs were chasing me, my legs ran till they
ached. A massive T-rex bent down to bite me,
then another smaller dinosaur bit my ankle. The
T-rex went to pounce ...
I woke up. It was just a dream! I stretched, to feel
my legs - they hurt and were bleeding ...

Angus Forsyth (10)
Hutton Rudby Primary School, Hutton Rudby

Scared

I was walking along the dark, abandoned road when, all of a sudden, I heard a scream! I turned my head to see what it was. I saw faint shadows walking behind the houses. The shadows got closer, someone grabbed me from behind! 'We've got you now,' they bellowed!

Olivia Brown (11)
Hutton Rudby Primary School, Hutton Rudby

Gunfire And Nightmares!

Blood! Guts! All over the battlefield. Deafening shots of gunfire sprinted over my head. Death-like screams of horror met my suffering ears as all I could hope for was your life not to be taken away from you. Then suddenly, *bang!* I was dead. *Gasp!* What a nightmare!

Piers Slade (10)
Hutton Rudby Primary School, Hutton Rudby

Santa

There was a jingle on the roof. It was Christmas.
Jack heard it. He slipped out of bed and opened
the window and scrambled onto the roof. He
slipped. Jack grabbed the gutter and pulled
himself up.
'There goes Santa.'
'Argh!' Jack screamed ... he was never seen again.

Cameron Twigg (10)
Hutton Rudby Primary School, Hutton Rudby

Nothing

'Yes!' shouted Andy. The ball was sky-blue, as round as an orange. It also had black markings. Danny kicked the ball over the swing, as well as kicking it through the window. 'Oh no!' shouted Danny.
'What's happened now?' Mum angrily shouted.
'Nothing,' mumbled Danny quietly.

Joseph Hughes (10)
Hutton Rudby Primary School, Hutton Rudby

Halloween Eve I

The vampires stay in on Halloween, this is why ...
'But why must *we* stay in? What about all the tasty human blood?' wailed Snort.
'For the last time, *no!*' boomed Mr Fang, 'go fetch Julliet!' But a gun fired, he was dead. To be continued ...

Mina Barthram (10)
Hutton Rudby Primary School, Hutton Rudby

A Sad Old Supper

Ugg picked up his spear, hurling it at the mammoth. The mammoth gave a mournful cry and dropped to the muddy ground, dead. Ugg smiled and ran to collect his supper. The mammoth looked as sad as a widow, blood oozing out of it, even Ugg felt a little sad.

Anna Fenwick (10)
Hutton Rudby Primary School, Hutton Rudby

A Close Escape

Ben was stampeding through the dark, musky forest. Evil branches attacked him with their whiplashing arms. His skin ripped. Blood raced down to the sodden ground. The treacherous beast gnashed its drooling jaws at Ben's leg. The predator was upon him!
Ben woke up in bed, paralysed with fear!

William Parry (10)
Hutton Rudby Primary School, Hutton Rudby

Scared Of Mice

The door creaked open, the tunnel beyond seemingly endless. Darkness and coldness surrounded them. Then they saw light. It was true, the shadow grew on the wall. Huge ears, giant fangs and long whiskers. 'Argh!' They screamed, turned and ran. The creature emerged from its lair - it was a mouse.

Jonathan Webster (10)
Hutton Rudby Primary School, Hutton Rudby

Dreaming

The pyramid had claimed her! For the millionth time Jill wondered if she would ever escape. She heard a sudden moan, she spun round. A mummy was coming towards her. Jill tried to scream but nothing came out ...

She woke up, she had survived ... it was only a ridiculous dream.

Andrew Sawer (10)

Hutton Rudby Primary School, Hutton Rudby

Scared

As Tim lay in bed he could hear the old oak tree tapping on the window. It was the middle of the night and he didn't dare whimper. *Bang! Crash! What was that?* Tim thought.
'It's only me!' he heard his sister call up the stairs.
'Phew!' he cried happily.

Sara Robinson (11)
Hutton Rudby Primary School, Hutton Rudby

The Dangers Of Football

Football is a great game, or so I thought. We had made it to the final. My team was winning. Only ten minutes to go. I was just about to score when two feet crashed into me. I fell to the floor. This is how I broke my leg.

Dominic Bennington (10)
Hutton Rudby Primary School, Hutton Rudby

Chased!

I darted breathlessly up the old cobbled path. He
was gaining on me! My heart pounded, faster and
faster. His hand reached out to grab me. 'Let me
go!' I screamed. I was shaking.
Suddenly ... I woke up. It was Mum.
'Wake up,' she urged, 'it's time for school.'

Emma Devereux (10)
Hutton Rudby Primary School, Hutton Rudby

Bonfire Night

In the distance I saw an old man sitting in a chair, enjoying a rare sunny day for November. Suddenly two mysterious men appeared. They picked the man up and put him on top of the bonfire. 'Stop! Stop!' I shouted and ran. 'It's Bonfire Night,' they said.

Jack Grimston (10)
Hutton Rudby Primary School, Hutton Rudby

The Nightmare Surprise

Howl, howl! I slowly turned to face my alarm clock. It was 3.30am. Quickly I went to see what was the matter with my dog, Tilly. I slowly tiptoed down the stairs. I opened the garage door and peeped in to see ... Tilly with three puppies snuggled up to her!

Phoebe Rennison (10)
Hutton Rudby Primary School, Hutton Rudby

A Trip To Legoland!

In the summer holiday this girl called Sophie went to Legoland. The first ride she went on was the tea cups. She really enjoyed all the rides. Before she knew it, it was time to go home, after an enjoyable day out.
On the way back she fell asleep.

Laura Hughes (9)
Hutton Rudby Primary School, Hutton Rudby

The Attic

Jack went to a sleepover. 'You're sleeping in the attic,' explained Sam. They got ready for bed. Jack got into bed and fell asleep. Suddenly he woke up. He saw a white shadow creeping around him. Jack turned the light on. *Phew!* It was only Sam's mum checking on him.

Lucy Sawer (9)
Hutton Rudby Primary School, Hutton Rudby

Talented Teenager

'I'm home Mum!' Charlie was a sharp, fit, sixteen-year-old. What was that? *Beep, beep!* A strange noise sounded from Dad's office. He crept in cautiously. The laptop read: 'GIS Global Intelligence Service'.

'We need you son. You're ready.' His parents were spies!

'Wow! I'm gonna be a spy?'

Morgan Burgess (9)

Hutton Rudby Primary School, Hutton Rudby

The Haunted House

Creak! There was a sudden noise, Tim didn't know where it came from. *Creak!* There it was again. Tim walked to the slimy door in front of him. He knew he was inside the haunted house. *Howl!* Tim knew it was a wolf!
'Huh!' It was a dream.

James Husband (10)
Hutton Rudby Primary School, Hutton Rudby

Bang!

Jim was at home watching a horror film. It was Halloween. He was scared. *Bang!* Jim woke up, his light switched on and off constantly. *Was it a ghost? 'Phew!'* Jim saw a book had fallen on his light. But was there something still there?

Alex Bourchier (9)

Hutton Rudby Primary School, Hutton Rudby

Dream

Tea bags, that's all Mum sent me to the shop for. I
just need to turn the corner, then I'm there!
I was just walking, then I felt cold, icy fingers
grabbing me. 'Help!' That's all I could say.
I woke up to the sound of my alarm ringing.

Lottie Senior (9)

Hutton Rudby Primary School, Hutton Rudby

My Killer!

Tim answered the door and a horrific sight met his eyes. It had big, evil eyes, a bloodstained squashy nose, curly orange hair, a multicoloured, striped costume, a murderous grin with etched-in smiles and ... 'Hang on a minute! You're a clown for my birthday! Come on in!'

Samuel Pearce (9)

Hutton Rudby Primary School, Hutton Rudby

The Adventure

Katie was in the garden when she saw a blue door. She had never seen it before so she went through it. It was another world! She walked and walked, over mountains, hills and lakes, then she saw a green door. She went through and ... she was back home!

Katie Thornton (10)
Hutton Rudby Primary School, Hutton Rudby

A Scary Night

One night a boy called Tom was fast asleep. Suddenly he heard a creak from the cellar and then ... *crack!* Tom emerged from his bed, it started to rain and lightning struck outside. The door swung open and revealed a cold, whimpering beast. 'Spot, my dog!'

Tom Readman (9)

Hutton Rudby Primary School, Hutton Rudby

The Evil Monster

The monster was big. He lived on my head. He was called Freddy. When Santa came he jumped on him and scratched him on his bottom. Santa got really angry and swung him round and round. He bashed him on his head with some bricks. They all lived happily after.

Ryan Whitlam (9)
Ings Primary School, Hull

The Magic Alien

There was an alien called Jongo, who was magic, everyone asked him if they could have a wish. But he said, 'No!'

So everyone was afraid apart from, one boy called Dom Littlewood. Bravely, he snuck into his house and stole his wishing wand and gave everyone a wish.

James Greendale (10)
Ings Primary School, Hull

The Old Man Living Next Door

There was an old man living next door. He had a long nose with beady eyes.
One night I heard a strange noise, it was very familiar. I thought it was the radio. I looked out of the window, it was the old man playing a big, shiny, new piano.

Abbie Everett (10)
Ings Primary School, Hull

Untitled

One day Santa Claus came to my house at night. I woke up and I crept downstairs. I got down just in time and I saw a red jacket and a beard and glasses. *Bang! Bang!* I jumped then I went into the lovely living room.

Leonnie Ashton (9)
Ings Primary School, Hull

The Man Living Next Door

Everyone knew he was in the gloomy house but
he lived in complete darkness.
Once a new family moved to the neighbourhood
and Mum knocked on the door. The door opened
but the man wasn't there. She stepped in. The
door closed with a slam. She never came back!

Katie Russell (10)
Ings Primary School, Hull

The Terrified Lady

One day an old lady got terrified in her house because some big kids burgled her. The old lady phoned the police. Then the police came to the house but the big kids ran off - the police tried to catch them, so the old lady was very happy.

Kimberley Page (10)
Ings Primary School, Hull

When The Blob Monster Attacked

'Argh! It's got me.' *Slap, slap.* 'Noo! Not me, please.' *Bang!* 'Shoot it! Shoot it!' *Slap, slap.* 'Gulp,' went the blob monster. *Baka, baka,* went the guns.
'Prepare the tanks!' shouted the commander. 'Bring in air force,' said a trooper. *Vroom!* In came the jets and bombed the place out.

Dylan Miles Ashley (9)
Ings Primary School, Hull

The Visit From Hell

There was a sharp knock on the door. I opened it. I got the shock of my life. It was the Devil from Hell! I thought I was dead for a moment. But it was real! Horns, fire and devilish laughter. I realised that it was Dad dressing up - again.

Edward Greaves (11)

Long Marston Primary School, Long Marston

The Flood

Whoosh! 'Argh!' The sea is roaring and vast, my ears sing with ear-piercing screeches, echoes fill the docks.
I'm preparing myself for the impact, trying to block out the harsh cries, when I hear a knock ... a voice!
'What are you doing?' exclaims the voice, 'you've flooded the bathroom.'

Abigail Coral Sayers (10)
Long Marston Primary School, Long Marston

Untitled

It was dark; owls hooted, rats squeaked. With a sharp knock at the door, her heart pounded, then she heard a long groan. Her hand went to grab the door handle. Her palms began to sweat, the door opened with a creak. A long, ghostly-white face then ... 'April Fools!'

Rhys Meredith (10)
Long Marston Primary School, Long Marston

Ninja Of Death

Hi, I'm Eddy or, as some people call me,
mad, stupid, invincible or just Eddy. I bet you
don't know my secret? Well I'll tell you. I am a
superhero, the Ninja of Death and I'm feared by
all bad guys. Hi ya!

Edward Telford (9)
Long Marston Primary School, Long Marston

Untitled

The Farrar family were mucking out except Cyril. He was playing football against the wall. Suddenly Meg barked, Dad started the tractor, Cyril crept in the dusty damp stable. He shouted, 'The cows are out of the yard!' Tom ran outside, but Cyril was joking in his cow costume. 'Moo!'

Thomas Farrar (9)

Long Marston Primary School, Long Marston

The Mysterious Shadow

'Argh! He's coming - the scary bear of the woods!'
laughed Fluffy the bunny. They both loved to play
magical games together. But then a shadow crept
up on them. What was it? They were scared stiff!
'Oh help!' screamed Fluffy, 'it's going to get us.'
'It's OK!' Joey reassured Fluffy.

Millie Crooks (10)
Mosborough Primary School, Sheffield

Mickey Mouse Surprise

Tom and Kitty were strolling when all of a sudden they caught sight of Mickey Mouse. 'What?' exclaimed Tom in surprise. As they looked back he was coming towards them. He whipped out two lollipops that were designed in swirly whirly and said, 'You are in Orlando, Disneyland!'

Megan Gilday (10)
Mosborough Primary School, Sheffield

Diabolical Goo

'Eww!' The diabolical goo was up to my chest and it was hard for me to breathe. It kept holding onto me for dear life as it rose to my shoulders. I managed to stretch my neck out far enough to reach my actual very last gasp of air.

Geri-Lee Madin (10)
Mosborough Primary School, Sheffield

Bully Wants A Friend

Beth was walking her small fluffy dog. Billy the bully came round the corner of the estate with his big fierce dog. She ran back to her house. Billy ran after her. She forgot to close the door so Billy went upstairs. He asked if she would be his friend.

Bradley Cooper (8)

Mosborough Primary School, Sheffield

Christmas Eve

On a cold dark Christmas Eve Max was tucked up in bed. He was terrified of Santa and Max was shaking. He was excited, hoping to receive presents. Santa was coming in the house and Max was awake. Max hid under the covers so Santa wouldn't see him in bed.

Ethan Medcraft (8)
Mosborough Primary School, Sheffield

Untitled

A lonely girl stood looking at all the rides. The girl was going to go on the haunted house ride. She was waiting in the line. She was sitting behind a bully, but the lonely girl was very brave, even though the bully went green and was very sick!

Ellie Unwin (8)

Mosborough Primary School, Sheffield

Pet Shop Grief

Fluffball, a lovely grey cat, and her kittens were asleep. It was 1 o'clock. Suddenly the cat woke up. Fluffball had a look around. She was panicking because Cookie had gone! Snowball and Fluffball looked everywhere. They looked in a small brown house and she appeared from round the back.

Ellys Firth (8)

Mosborough Primary School, Sheffield

Untitled

Jamie went in the spooky forest to see her friends but nobody was there. Jamie started to become scared. The next minute there was a flash! She fell to the ground.

'Oh no,' said a voice. She jumped up but it was only her brother!

Paige Prescott (8)
Mosborough Primary School, Sheffield

Splash!

Splash! A huge wave went through the pool as Ben's thirteen-stone dad jumped into the cold, blue water. Ben wanted to follow, but was so terrified he started to cry. Ben's mother comforted him and put his armbands on. 'Don't worry, I'll help you Ben. I've booked swimming lessons.'

May Thompson (8)
Mosborough Primary School, Sheffield

Amy Alone

Amy is lost in a wood, at 3 o'clock. She thinks she is alone but she is not. Suddenly she hears a deafening noise. She is wondering what it is. Amy sees something. It is only a cute cat that got stuck.

Caitlin Collins (8)
Mosborough Primary School, Sheffield

Crash!

Crash! Amy landed on Mars! She stepped out of the shiny spaceship and looked at the twinkling stars around her. Then a slimy green monster crept up on her and roared fiercely. She hid behind her spaceship. Then the monster spotted her and ran into her spaceship, fast.

Olivia Lees (8)
Mosborough Primary School, Sheffield

A Horrific Sight

Jane opened the creaky doors of the cinema. She smelt the delicious smell of popcorn. A sudden creak came from the doors. 'I'm sure my friends are here,' Jane said. A strange figure started to walk near her. 'Please get away!'
'Surprise,' her friends laughed.

Lauren Hancock (8)
Mosborough Primary School, Sheffield

Take A Dip

Sarah shivered as the strict swimming teacher threatened to push her in the pool. She screamed for her mum but she had already gone. Sarah kicked her legs as the teacher pushed her in. Then she came to the surface, then she realised she could swim!

Lucy Bacon (8)
Mosborough Primary School, Sheffield

Gino Scared To Death

Gino was walking down the old crooked path on his own. Gino was so scared he said, 'I am never coming here again.' Then Gino spotted an ancient park with dirty slides and a broken climbing frame. Then the gates closed! Gino climbed over the gate and went home, safely.

Charlie Crooks (8)

Mosborough Primary School, Sheffield

Untitled

It was a freezing cold day. A young boy at the North Pole looked around. There were lots of furry, white polar bears, slimy fish and melting icebergs. The next day the boy noticed all of the ice was under the water. 'Oh, I'm moving to Spain!'

Taya Dawson (8)
Mosborough Primary School, Sheffield

The Pet Fish Shop

A small girl named Daisy, with black hair and brown eyes, wanted a fish, so she went to the pet fish shop. The shop was crowded. The shopkeeper let Daisy catch the fish, but she couldn't. The shopkeeper caught them. Daisy called them Goldy the goldfish, Snowball and Finny.

Charlotte Morris (8)
Mosborough Primary School, Sheffield

Crash! Bang! Wallop!

An alien ship was flying in space. Suddenly a meteor shot out of nowhere and hit the alien ship. It exploded so fast it caught fire on the way down. *Crash! Bang! Wallop!* A green-eyed alien collapsed and died. His body was used for medical research.

Joshua Nolan (8)
Mosborough Primary School, Sheffield

The Terrible Accident

Aleysha went to the ice-skating rink with her family. She got her skates on. She fell and landed on her arm, cutting it.
Aleysha was rushed to the nearest hospital. She was finally awoken by the doctor. The doctor told her that she had fractured her arm badly.

Millicent Andrews (8)
Mosborough Primary School, Sheffield

Scary Dinner Time!

At dinner time Amy went into the dark and spooky classroom to get something. When she tried to get a book out, the bully, called Bob, stood behind her about to scare her. Just then Amy's teacher walked in and put the light on. The next day Bob was ill.

Faith Taylor (8)
Mosborough Primary School, Sheffield

Spooky

One spooky night in a school on Halloween, a young boy called Jack ate too many sweeties. Jack had a daydream. In his daydream, glowing ghosts were surrounding him. Blood-red zombies and spooky bats and red goblins. Then he realised it was all a daydream.

Daniel Bradshaw (8)
Mosborough Primary School, Sheffield

Water Wave

When a blonde-haired girl called Jane was playing,
a huge wave hit her boat. She looked up. Jane
looked at the floor, it was soaking. 'It's going to
sink,' Jane said. She noticed the floor was wet
because the wave had made a hole. She stuck
planks over it.

Stephen Heslip (8)
Mosborough Primary School, Sheffield

Jumped!

'Wow!' Lucy's mum jumped in the swimming pool and then Lucy jumped in with her mum. Her dad said, 'Do you want an ice cream?'
'Yes I do.' Lucy got out of the swimming pool but she dropped her ice cream in the pool, just trying to be cool.

Alicia Nadin (8)
Mosborough Primary School, Sheffield

Fairyland

Daisy was playing in her garden when she noticed a wooden door in her tree and a rusty key in a lock. She turned the key and there was Fairyland. It was beautiful. A fairy came up to her and said, 'Hello, welcome to Fairyland, follow me.'

Jessie-Ann Pinder (8)
Mosborough Primary School, Sheffield

Crazy School

I went to school music in the hall. I went in. *Wow! Swimming pool. Wow! Dance mat*. My teacher was in her bikini in a Jacuzzi. My school is great! Mr Holland, dancing. I can't believe it. A party, I love parties! I love school.

Hannah Brown (8)
Mosborough Primary School, Sheffield

Different House

I was walking home from school - I crept into the house. I knew we were throwing a surprise party for my little sister. I went into the backyard, they were already having a party. 'Hi! Welcome to the party.'
Hang on - *I don't even know these people!*

Morgan Wilson (8)
Mosborough Primary School, Sheffield

Surprised By Grandma

Every day Kylie went to visit her grandma. She walked into the rest home. *This isn't the rest home!* The next thing she knew she was in space. She explored around.

'Surprise!' her granny wheeled out. What a day!

Robert Stirrup (9)

Mosborough Primary School, Sheffield

Cookies!

Charlotte opened the door, the classroom door. The cupboard doors were falling off and the chairs were on their backs. Charlotte looked around the classroom. She opened the stock-cupboard door; there was a cookie monster! Charlotte screamed! The monster looked at Charlotte, 'I only look for cookies!'

Sophie Clarkson (9)
Mosborough Primary School, Sheffield

Clock Attack

Jack walked through the lonely corridor. *Bang!*
'What was that?' said Jack. Then some of the clocks came alive and spat their hands towards him. 'Nooooo!' cried Jack.
Then he remembered he was asleep. 'Argh!' gasped Jack. Then the door opened. 'Nooooo!' The clocks were back!

Max Nicholson Stubbs (9)
Mosborough Primary School, Sheffield

Untitled

Today on 'News At 10', there was a serious
robbery at Primark. It was a disaster, no one
knows who it was. Police ran after him. He stole
one diamond, two brand new delicate watches
and three fragile pots.
A girl had a scary dream.

Amelia Ward (8)
Mosborough Primary School, Sheffield

Untitled

The bank looked different because it had been robbed. There was nobody there. She walked through the robbed bank. She saw a shadow. She was scared. But it was a joke. 'Surprise! It's your birthday!'

Tilly Moore (8)

Mosborough Primary School, Sheffield

The Horrible Hall

As Lucy walked into the school hall, it was horrible. There were spiders and cobwebs up the wall and it was all dusty and there was even haunting music. She could hear wolves howling. 'This really is not nice,' said Lucy. Phew, it was only the exciting school Halloween disco!

Emily Daynes (9)
Mosborough Primary School, Sheffield

The Playground

Ding! went the bell. I stepped outside, I started bouncing. What was happening? I was getting higher and higher - where was everybody? *I must be in space. Ow! What was that?* It felt like netting. *Wow!* My eyes opened. Oh, we were playing blind man's bluff on the trampoline.

Gemma Heslip (9)
Mosborough Primary School, Sheffield

Pay Back

On the 26th November 1941, it was finally true, Anne Frank found Adolf Hitler. He was hiding in a massive annexe. He was sent to a police station near the centre of Berlin. Anne Frank was taking over the world! How many more people would she find?

Rhys Brown (9)
Mosborough Primary School, Sheffield

Vellog's Attack

Zara sensed someone behind her. She turned around and screamed! Vellog the mighty phantom towered above her, his nine eyes glaring at her. Zara screamed again, but there was nobody there to hear her. She looked down, suddenly horrified to see herself turning to stone. Zara had become a statue!

Annabel Reeder (9)
Mosborough Primary School, Sheffield

No Pressure

It was 2-2 on penalties. I needed to score. I had butterflies in my tummy, the whole team was counting on me. My dad was cheering in the crowd. If I missed my team would lose, *the quarter finals!* I finally stepped up for the penalty. The whistle blew ...

Joseph Bell (9)
Mosborough Primary School, Sheffield

Untitled

I was having the time of my life! I was excited but a little nervous. I leapt from the boat and was surrounded by coral! Suddenly the air was filled with screams. I looked around and saw a fish coming towards me with an enormous mouth. I was petrified.

Georgia O'Connor (9)
Mosborough Primary School, Sheffield

Only A Stone's Throw Away

'Alfie, close the curtains!' I shouted. There were a number of teenagers lurking outside. Suddenly a stone came flying towards the open window and crashed on Matthew's head! Matthew was out cold!

One hour later Matthew awoke, 'Where am I?'

Callum Cresswell (9)
Mosborough Primary School, Sheffield

Horror

It was war, I knew I wouldn't survive another day. I knew I would get killed, but I had to live, I had to! Suddenly I looked up and all I could see was darkness, but then I finally found it was all just a dream.

Sophie Ayres (9)
Mosborough Primary School, Sheffield

The Mystery Sweets

The shop stood in darkness for the night.
In the morning it opened for the day as usual,
but all the sweets were gone! The shop owner
gazed outside and saw them scattered around the
horses' field. The owner looked on as the horses
gobbled them down!

Sarah Bain (9)
Mosborough Primary School, Sheffield

The Slide Of Doom

Annabel soared down the slide and was catapulted into the air. She crashed into a pile of leaves and dropped into a hole! Diggers tried to get her out but they couldn't. Nobody saw her again, until a girl came along and found a secret hole. She was saved.

Imogen Percival (9)
Mosborough Primary School, Sheffield

In The Snow

One day it was very snowy. So I went outside.
It was freezing. As I walked all I could hear was
crunch, crunch. I bumped into some friends, we
all built a giant snowman. Then suddenly he came
to life! We played all day with him, but then he
melted.

Amy Hannah (9)
Mosborough Primary School, Sheffield

The Money Machine

The Money Machine was the most feared criminal in the whole of Europe until one night in the middle of December. It was stealing £300,000,000 from the Bank of England, when the security guards found out. They chased it away but it still managed to get away with £200,000,000!

Sam Saunderson (9)
Mosborough Primary School, Sheffield

Nascar Racing

I was dreaming about Nascar in my bed. Next
minute, I was driving in one!
Two laps to the end of the race. The car behind me
blows a tyre so I have an advantage. Yippee! I've not
had a pitstop in ages, I've done it! I've won! Yay!

Jordan Stimely (9)
Mosborough Primary School, Sheffield

Untitled

I was riding a bike in an alleyway when I heard a noise. I looked behind me very quickly - it was nobody. I carried on riding. Then I heard a bang. I quickly rode towards the noise. There was a person laid on the floor, dead!

Melissa Middleton (9)
Mosborough Primary School, Sheffield

Birthday

It was the day before my birthday. My best friend
Georgia was sleeping over. After eating many
Maltesers, we finally fell asleep. Suddenly Georgia
jumped out of bed. 'Did you hear that?'
We crept downstairs, 'Surprise!' I was bombarded
with gifts!

Laura Brown (9)
Mosborough Primary School, Sheffield

Christmas Is Coming

On the 25th December, Christmas Day, Jacob was making a snowman in the back garden. After he finished he went to fetch his mum to have a look at it. Once she arrived, she did not believe him. 'But Mum, I'm sure!' The snowman had gone!

Olivia Barnsley (9)
Mosborough Primary School, Sheffield

Untitled

The goalkeeper was getting ready for the shot.
Wayne Rooney was always ready for this kind of
set-piece, he stepped up and had a shot and it
flew into the top left-hand corner. That was it,
they had won! Manchester United had won! They
had really done it.

Luca Montisci (9)
Mosborough Primary School, Sheffield

Let's Go

It was an hour till the race. Harry was ready. Just then he noticed he was missing a brake. Joe ran nervously to collect the missing part! Within a flash he was back. Harry stared at his enemy who'd bullied him for so long. The lights flashed red, red, green ...

Harry Hudson (9)

Mosborough Primary School, Sheffield

She's Dying

The sand tickled her feet. Kate was okay, but she didn't want to leave. She walked calmly down the sea thinking about how much fun she'd had at Florida Shores. She'd lived there all her life and wouldn't be coming back - ever again. Kate was dying, but of unnatural causes ...

Emily Wilson (10)
Mosborough Primary School, Sheffield

The Capture

One day there was a curious crab that lay still on an old rusted pipe in a rock pool. Suddenly a boy stomped over to the old broken rock pool with a colossal fishing net. 'Oh no, what shall I do?' screamed the crab at the top of his voice.

Nathan Higgins (10)
Mosborough Primary School, Sheffield

Angel Vs Devil

Finally, thought the Devil, *I will spread pitch-blackness all over the world ... Kaboom! What?* The army of the angels had come to take him down. 'Evil spirits! Attack!' The angels got their crossbows and, with expert aim, took the spirits down. The lead angel then slaughtered the evil Devil.

Adam Hague (10)
Mosborough Primary School, Sheffield

Different Way

Ring, ring, rang my alarm on Monday morning. I went downstairs and saw a letter on the kitchen table. It said that my mum and dad had gone to work. So I did everything I needed to do and set off, but a different way. Then, I met the monster!

Isabelle Cartwright (9)
Mosborough Primary School, Sheffield

Pirate Pete's Bloody Adventure

Pirate Pete was arriving home when the guards caught him and took all his treasure and locked him up.
The next day Pete combed his beard and lined up for his execution. When it was Pete's turn he knelt down and his head was chopped off and everyone went home.

Callum Neenan (10)
Mosborough Primary School, Sheffield

The Dog

The dog ran quickly through fields and as the men chased him the men caught him. He growled angrily like a storm getting ready to strike. The men dragged him to their old rusty van, which on the side said, 'Dog Catchers'. What was going to happen to the dog?

Olivia Timms (10)
Mosborough Primary School, Sheffield

The Angry Boy

Once there was an angry boy. He never felt happy. He didn't like doing anything. Harry managed to smile but never laughed, consequently he didn't have one friend! His family didn't care about him and every day he was bored and angry until, he found a friend!

Callum Turner (10)
Mosborough Primary School, Sheffield

Tiger Hunter

Bang ... it was too late, he had killed the poor creature. Eyes were all pointed at the lion. For a few seconds no one spoke. The hunter saw his chance and legged it to the jungle - by now villagers were out of their homes and running.

Rosie-Mae Pinder (9)

Mosborough Primary School, Sheffield

Disaster Strikes!

'Watch out below!' cried Daz. *Boom!* 'What the heck just happened?'
'I have no idea,' screamed Prince. It was World War II in Germany.
'What shall we do now, we have lost half of our men?' cried Daz.
'I think we should retreat now.' But it was too late.

Laurence Pickford (10)
Mosborough Primary School, Sheffield

Fat Fish Fire!

The fat fish was walking down the winding road when he saw a small house on fire. The fish tapped on the door, but no one answered. He climbed in the nearby open window. The red hot fire was everywhere. Suddenly the fish caught fire and then he was dead!

Lois Spencer (10)
Mosborough Primary School, Sheffield

Snatched!

The innocent child walked along the seashore with her parents. She was on holiday in Greece. The girl ran happily towards the sea in excitement. She jumped into the water with her father's back turned. There was a deafening scream. Her father quickly turned around. The girl was gone!

Erin Rhodes (10)
Mosborough Primary School, Sheffield

The Potato

The lonely potato lived under the mud and rocks. He liked it there. One dull, rainy and stormy day a farmer called Bill came outside with his big shovel when it was raining. Consequently, Bill the farmer got wet. He dug into the ground and unfortunately squashed the poor potato.

Tyler Goodwin (9)
Mosborough Primary School, Sheffield

The Competition

The hyperactive hamster was juggling away to his new music while he was on stilts. The children thought it was absolutely bonkers. However, the adults weren't so crazy, they were booing him off! The hamster only just got through to the next round (I don't think the adults were happy).

Jack Farnsworth (10)
Mosborough Primary School, Sheffield

The Moon

There the moon lay waiting for the sun to come in and for him to go out. His job wasn't very hard really, all he had to do was make the sky a bit bright so people could see. The sun had the difficult job until, the day disappears.

Joshua Ball (10)
Mosborough Primary School, Sheffield

Into The Menacing

Bang! James shot him dead. All of a sudden a dark figure covered the eerie room. James sprinted as fast as he could. He got into his car. Suddenly he took his shaking hands off the out-of-control steering wheel and collided, veering towards the edge of the cliff!

Joshua Birtles (11)
Mosborough Primary School, Sheffield

Am I Dead?

Out went the lights. The back door unlocked. Sarah reached to close it. *Kaboom!* She was lifeless on the floor. Four mysterious figures came through the door. 'Plant it there!'
'OK - we have one minute until it explodes. We need to get out now!' Sarah slowly reached out to him ...

Dempsey Moore (10)
Mosborough Primary School, Sheffield

The Powerplant Reactor

'It's going to blow!' The alarm bellowed out as the core started to crack. Armoured vehicles arrived at the powerplant. A man went over to the boss and asked, 'How many people have got out?'
'A hundred, but there's still some inside!'
'Can you get them out?'
'I'll try.'

Joshua Lilleker (11)
Mosborough Primary School, Sheffield

The Treacherous Tempting Temple

Bang! Right on time. The mysterious meteorite whisked me away to the Toadstool Temple. I cautiously crept into the palace. In a flash, fungi grenades were being launched. 'I've nearly got the holy fungus!' Suddenly mushroom gods appeared and with some salt they were on fire and I was safe.

George Cheetham (11)
Mosborough Primary School, Sheffield

My Death!

Bang! The bullet whistled past my head. *Crash!* Another bullet fractionally missed my ear and sped into the trenches. I reached for my gun but I couldn't find it. A third bullet arced towards me. I was dead? Wasn't I?
'Max, get up! It's time for school, you're late again.'

Alex Brown (11)
Mosborough Primary School, Sheffield

Baa Baa Blue Sheep

Baa Baa Blue Sheep was trotting into a meadow, when sudden, *crash!* He stumbled into a huge hole. Immediately he heard a crack! He broke his hoof. 'Ouch, Baa Baa!' shouted Baa Baa Blue Sheep. No one was there to help him. 'Help me!'

'That's Baa Baa Blue Sheep!'

'Baa!'

Chloe Dawson (10)
Mosborough Primary School, Sheffield

Shaun The Sheep

It's Shaun the sheep, he looks around for sheep that cannot bleep. He loves to play inside some hay and mucks around all of the day. He loves his greens but he really hates his peas. It's Shaun the sheep. That is what he loves!

Grace Akers (11)
Mosborough Primary School, Sheffield

My Quest That Never Ended

I'd done it. My quest was over. I'd triumphed again. I fled happily for the door. Only it swung shut too early. I was enclosed in the deep darkness. A black pit stood before me. Suddenly I slipped and fell in, squealing silently. Only to awake on my bedroom floor.

Skye Wilson (10)
Mosborough Primary School, Sheffield

All Swallowed Up!

It's everywhere! Swallowing, chewing me up. Where am I? I can't remember. It's so long since I breathed cool, fresh air. It grows a little every day, but when will the air run out? It's so smelly. I'm so, so lonely. I'd rather die than stay here a minute longer.

Sophie Ryan-Marrison (10)
Mosborough Primary School, Sheffield

The Day I Met Death

I was fast asleep on Friday the 13th - a *crash!* Then a *bang!* The noise came from the next room. I cautiously crept towards the room, it was standing about five yards away. Its green, sapphire, piercing eyes blazed at me. Therefore I knew I was going to die ...

Darius Thomas (10)
Mosborough Primary School, Sheffield

Secret Surprise

He walked along the spooky floor. Nervously he opened the door. *Tick-tock* went the grandfather clock as it struck midnight. The handle creaked as he twisted it. Uncomfortably he looked around the room. He saw a weird bookshelf. Suddenly everyone jumped from a cupboard; it was his birthday!

Simeon Janvier (10)
Our Lady & St Joseph's Catholic Primary School, Rotherham

Out At Night!

The cold damaged my brain as I approached the house. I was starting to go like ice, my friend pushed the door handle down. In the house it was dark and gloomy as my family all jumped out and shouted, 'Surprise!' We all had a fabulous birthday party.

Brooke Goddard (10)

Our Lady & St Joseph's Catholic Primary School, Rotherham

Lost Hope

I walked through the woods, the wind whistled through the trees. Suddenly I saw a shadow. I turned round, just then I heard footsteps coming my way. *Phew,* it was a little dog, galloping along the path. I leaned down to stroke it, its fur was as soft as velvet.

Sophie Walker (11)
Our Lady & St Joseph's Catholic Primary School, Rotherham

The Beastly Bedroom

Holly pulled the covers over her head as she heard a loud hiss. She felt something warm crawl over her stomach. Suddenly she heard her alarm clock beeping. 'Mum! The cat's on my bed again,' said Holly.

'You silly cat, I've told you about this, now get down!' said Mum.

Evie Brakes (10)

Our Lady & St Joseph's Catholic Primary School, Rotherham

The Alien Mask

Alice sat nervously on the edge of the designer sofa. 'I wonder when Mum will be home?' she said to her dog, Lucky. There was a loud knock at the door. She screamed. It was an alien with an evil dark eye.

'Surprise!' *Phew*, it was her brother!

Melissa Winder (11)

Our Lady & St Joseph's Catholic Primary School, Rotherham

The Darkness

Nervously he was led out of the car. Peter's blindfold was taken off and standing in front of him was the airport. He had no idea that he was going on a surprise holiday to Dubai. He jumped with excitement at the thought of a stunningly beautiful, sandy, palm beach.

Jai Barber (7)

Our Lady & St Joseph's Catholic Primary School, Rotherham

Santa In The Kitchen

When Charlie came down the stairs, underneath
the tree there were lots of presents. Charlie was
so excited about tomorrow because he could
open his presents. But then he noticed that Santa
was in the kitchen. So, quietly, he crept upstairs
and went back to bed and fell asleep.

Debbie Cocking (8)
Our Lady & St Joseph's Catholic Primary School, Rotherham

Bad Dream

On Christmas Day I went downstairs and there were no presents. I ran back upstairs and told my mum and dad that Father Christmas hadn't been, when I heard my name called out. 'Hollie, Hollie, wake up!' my mum and dad said. I was having a bad dream.

Hollie Roddis (8)

Our Lady & St Joseph's Catholic Primary School, Rotherham

New School

John was really worried on his first day at school. He missed his old school and friends. No way would the new one be as good. Then he met funny Edward who showed him around and he felt better. John thought, *maybe it'll be OK after all!*

Luke Morris (7)
Our Lady & St Joseph's Catholic Primary School, Rotherham

A Leafal Walk In The Park

The park seemed deserted. Ashly entered, thinking she was about to have a great day. As Ashly turned round, she saw a pile of leaves. Suddenly one of them sat up and started talking! Before she could blink a man with a leaf blower sucked them up. What a *releaf!*

Alexandra Beal (10)

Our Lady & St Joseph's Catholic Primary School, Rotherham

The Next Door Neighbour's Dog

Sam began walking to school when a fierce dog
chased her all the way home. 'Mum! Mum!'
'What?'
'There's a dog chasing me.'
A bang on the door. 'Oh no!' she cried, 'it's the
dog.' She opened the door and ... it turned out to
be the next door neighbour's dog.

Cerris Robinson (11)
Our Lady & St Joseph's Catholic Primary School, Rotherham

Nightmares Are Bad

The darkness crept around the old house. The spirits rushed through, room to room. Alex stood at the door waiting for somebody to answer. Nothing. Then the door opened. Alex looked nervous. He stepped in. The door then shut. Suddenly a man was behind him. The gun was fired. *Argh!*

Ryan Appleton (11)

Ralph Butterfield Primary School, Haxby

What Happened?

Max could sense danger. There was someone or something coming. *Crack!* Max stopped still. He looked all around him. He was somewhere, but where? He closed his eyes and wished he was somewhere else. But it was no use and there, right in front of him, was ... *oh no!*

Emily Cooper
Ralph Butterfield Primary School, Haxby

In The Forest!

As high as the tallest giant, the spooky trees loomed menacingly above a terrified Claire. She screamed a long, petrified scream. Gasping for breath, Claire fell to the muddy ground. The lion pounced. It licked her cold face - she glared around her own garden as her cat leapt at her.

Dana-Claire Headley (10)
Ralph Butterfield Primary School, Haxby

Clickety-Clack Along The Track

Creaking, clattering, the cart moved slowly up the track. Smoke drifted, unfurling Bella's vision; as it cleared, a translucent ghost glided through her head, giving the feeling of being plunged into icy water. *Argh!* Pearly-white canines sank into her pale skin ... light shone at the end of the ride.

Emily Burchell (11)
Ralph Butterfield Primary School, Haxby

Bang! Bang!

Bang! Bang! Bang! Joe ran. It was following him, firing its gun. Turning a corner, he found a dead end. He was done for. It came and fired. *Game Over!*

Holly Bamford (11)
Ralph Butterfield Primary School, Haxby

Darkness

The impenetrable darkness clawed at Jack, as he sprinted into the gloom! Entering the crumbling house, silhouettes swam in and out of his mind, attacking him. Pain tore his head apart; he didn't know why! Jack turned back, his path was blocked by a ghostly figure. The end had begun ...

Owen Lambert (11)
Ralph Butterfield Primary School, Haxby

The Women

Spiders dangled, wind howled and thunder blasted as I stared at the tall woman. My hair blew as her breath hung over me. I was scared. Her hand came out and onto my shaking shoulder. 'Hi Nan,' I whispered. But then ...

Jenni-Rose Ashby (10)
Ralph Butterfield Primary School, Haxby

A Bad Dream

I swam and swam to the top of the murky water.
Something was after me, lurking around at the
bottom. Suddenly I turned around. 'Argh!' I
screamed. A huge creepy animal smacked my
face. Petrified, I was hit again harder.
'C'mon honey, it's morning,' moaned my mum
slapping me, cruelly.

Millie O'Sullivan (10)
Ralph Butterfield Primary School, Haxby

The Plunge!

Gasping for breath, I flung my arms and legs around my stunned body. Wrapping around me, cool and clear, the ferocious water roared past my sensitive ears. Clutching me close, the angry lion ran its large paws through my tangled brown hair. 'Fabulous Millie! What a superb dive, absolutely amazing!'

Amy Brown (11)
Ralph Butterfield Primary School, Haxby

The Gun

Peering round the corner, a shadow slickly slid along the wall. Then Bob pulled out his magnum. Suddenly a masked man smashed through the window, wielding a gun. Bob spun, peeking over the top of the table. *Ping, ping!* Bullets bounced off the table.

'Damn, I'm out of money!'

Cameron Beresford (11)
Ralph Butterfield Primary School, Haxby

Trapped!

Creak! Slowly, the rusty door locked. Henry was alone with only his baby brother to accompany him. They were trapped where no one would dare to go. His brother, Sean, was overjoyed but Henry was petrified. They were trapped - in Babies 'R' Us!

Thomas Mulholland (10)

Ralph Butterfield Primary School, Haxby

It's Coming

Bang! Bang! Sam's terror was coming! Buckets of sweat poured down his face. His worst nightmare was happening. *Creak!* The door slowly opened but Sam couldn't retreat any further. The monster had won. His granny's wrinkly face came into view. *No!* Sam had been given a horrid, slobbery kiss.

James Murray (11)
Ralph Butterfield Primary School, Haxby

Ghostly Halls

Creeping slowly down the hall, a stick leg touched Bella's bumpy arm. Cobwebs hung watching, as smoke poured out of a little room in the corner. (But was it smoke?) Drip-dropping water knocked on the trapdoor. 'Help!' As the figure approached, Bella realised this was the end!

Georgia McMahon (11)
Ralph Butterfield Primary School, Haxby

The Rider!

Creeping through the shadows, absorbing everyone who came near. At night he rode a black dragon. It was night. A kid ran by. He stepped onto the path. All the lights went out! The kid stopped. The rider approached, grabbed him. His dragon betrayed him! '*Argh!*'

Benjamin Smythe (10)
Ralph Butterfield Primary School, Haxby

70 Million

Crack! The prehistoric rock split open. Out wandered a gooey ball, while little bits of blood dripped out. It crawled around like an ant. Every now and then it would stumble. It could eat a deer at such an age. And everyone thought he was extinct.

Sam Emmott (11)
Ralph Butterfield Primary School, Haxby

The Library

One day in a dark room, in a dark library in a dark city, someone lingered, waiting. I walked in and stood, my heart raced. I thought to myself, *what should I do?* I walked further in. Someone grabbed me … and kissed me. It was Mum!

Francesca McShane (10)
Reeth & Gunnerside Primary Confederation, Richmond

A Nasty Surprise

One day a boy called Tom went into a church and said, 'Anybody there?' and there was no reply. But when he said it again there was a reply from behind a door. He looked behind the door and saw an alive skeleton. *Oh no!*

Daniel Johnson (9)
Reeth & Gunnerside Primary Confederation, Richmond

Mission Mars

Marty found a rocket at NASA. There was an alien aboard. It was called Steve. They made friends and they decided to fly to Mars. Steve pushed the big red button and the rocket took off. They landed on Mars. Steve saw his family. Marty had reunited Steve and family.

Nicholas Lanier (10)
Reeth & Gunnerside Primary Confederation, Richmond

The Wolfenstein

The professor gave his evil laugh a try when he saw his supernatural gene experiment had bolts of electricity running through it. Then a growl escaped from its mouth and a fist smashed the chain. The ungainly beast crashed through the wall.

Wolfenstein was born.

Nathan Thorpe (11)

Reeth & Gunnerside Primary Confederation, Richmond

The Noise

The door burst open, the leaves swirled around the passage. Distant screams could be heard as the misty night grew darker and colder in the small village. Nancy came bursting in and shouted, 'Hello? Hello?' but nobody answered. Then she heard a strange noise from upstairs. What could it be?

Syd Dawson (10)
Reeth & Gunnerside Primary Confederation, Richmond

Spook School

I walked down the dark corridor, my heart was beating fast, it felt like it was going to pop out of my chest. As I reached the tall figure, I realised it was just an old sheet on a door.

Harry Potter (10)

Reeth & Gunnerside Primary Confederation, Richmond

The Horror Park

Once there was a haunted theme park which
nobody went to. Every time somebody went in,
they disappeared. There were some rockets but
every time anyone went on, they disappeared.
Nobody knew where they had gone.
Then one day a news team went in but were
never heard of again.

Matthew Short (9)
Reeth & Gunnerside Primary Confederation, Richmond

The Rotten Smell

The smell was awful, it smelt like rotten eggs. My nostrils burned, the smell would never go away. It travelled all around the house. I looked down and saw this putrid vomit-inducing mass.
I hate changing my brother's nappy!

Emily Russell (10)
Reeth & Gunnerside Primary Confederation, Richmond

Mistake

'Ouch!' the boy cried. He had tripped over
something. Something wet, soggy and disgusting.
He leant down to feel what it was. *'Yuck!'* he
complained.
He heard voices, one voice seemed to be that of
his mother. 'How many times do you have to be
told to tidy your bedroom?'

Daniel Roberts (10)

Reeth & Gunnerside Primary Confederation, Richmond

Toasted Alive!

Holly woke up. She smelt smoke. *Argh,* she thought, *fire!* She crept up and opened her door a crack. She tiptoed down the stairs wondering where the smell was coming from. She stopped, smoke was coming from the kitchen.
'*Argh!*' screamed her mum, 'I've trapped my finger in the toaster!'

Connie Smith (11)
Reeth & Gunnerside Primary Confederation, Richmond

My Bedroom

Oh dear, I thought, Mum was going inside my
bedroom.
'*Wow!*' she cried. I gave her a strange look. Inside,
my robot was resting in a clean tidy room. 'You
can have all your friends over for Christmas.'
I sighed happily, this was going to be a great
Christmas!

Charis Pain (10)
Reeth & Gunnerside Primary Confederation, Richmond

The Noise

Emily was walking along the pavement on a gloomy dark night. She kept hearing noises. She turned around and saw nothing. Emily started running. She heard the noise again. She looked over her shoulder. There was a bus coming and mysteriously, just like that, it vanished!
'Very strange,' whispered Emily.

Georgia Hird (10)

Reeth & Gunnerside Primary Confederation, Richmond

Hunted

I came out of the forest with my squadron,
frightened, cold and out of ammo. We were
surrounded by the enemy, defeated! They caught
us and put us in a prisoner-of-war camp.
It took us six months to escape and now I tell you
the tale. Free! Safe!

Sean Nicholson (10)

Reeth & Gunnerside Primary Confederation, Richmond

Trapped!

I pushed the game into the console - a bolt of
electricity shot up my arm. I fell backwards.
When I got up I realised I was in the game.
Trapped!
I started to panic, I heard Mum shouting.
Suddenly someone was shaking me, it was Mum.
I had been dreaming.

Ben Wilkinson (7)

Reeth & Gunnerside Primary Confederation, Richmond

Deathbed Of Hell

I wake up, see something, someone chuckling in
my face, shaking me violently. Their breath smells
of sour apples. I push them away but they're
far too strong for me. Should I call for Mum?
No, she's asleep. I struggle until; 'Wake up, it's
Christmas!' cries my older sister, Jess!

Hannah Egan (10)
St Margaret's CE Primary School, Horsforth

ET Goes Home

Elliot and ET rode on the bike to the forest. ET had said the spaceship would land here. They arrived just as the ship was landing. The lights shut down and the door swung open with a thunderous crash! Then suddenly, his mother walked out. 'ET your tea's ready!'

Daniel Baghban (11)

St Margaret's CE Primary School, Horsforth

The Unknown Knocker

Emily dumped her bags on the sofa. It had been another horrible day. But suddenly there was a knock on the door. 'Come in,' said Emily. There was no reply. Emily opened the door and no one was there.

'Surprise!'

Still no one. Then she screamed ...

Lucy Knight (9)

Sand Hutton CE Primary School, Sand Hutton

The Dark Cellar

I had to go to my uncle's house. Well, it's more like a castle. When I got there I went down some steps into the cellar, then I saw a dark shadow loom towards me. It was only Sooty, my uncle's cat. 'Hey do you want to go to McDonald's?'

Freya Whiteside (9)
Skelton Newby Hall CE Primary School, Skelton-on-Ure

Some Adventure

Once there were two robots named R4 and R5.
That day R4 wanted to go on an adventure.
'OK,' said R5.
When they got into a forest, they saw two small
animals. The animals followed the robots until,
'*Run!* That's enough of an adventure for one day!'

Benjamin Needham (9)
Skelton Newby Hall CE Primary School, Skelton-on-Ure

When I Went Swimming

I get to the swimming baths. I get changed in the girls' changing room and put my cap on. I get ready and the man says, 'Go!' I jump in the water, swimming as fast as I can go. I get to the end and I've won a gold medal!

Abigail James (7)

Skelton Newby Hall CE Primary School, Skelton-on-Ure

The Killer Cat!

One cold snowy day Holly took her dog for a walk in the wood. Entering the wood she heard a *grrrr* noise! Holly was scared now. *Grrrr* went the noise again. Holly looked up - it was Mrs Dun's cat!

'How did you get there? I'll take you home.'

Ellen Gill (8)

Skelton Newby Hall CE Primary School, Skelton-on-Ure

Maple's Great Escape!

Maple was a dog but she had a secret; she liked to roam free. Today was the day she would escape. She looked at the wall. She ran, she jumped, she somersaulted right over the wall. She'd made it! What would she do next?

Jakob Faass (8)
Skelton Newby Hall CE Primary School, Skelton-on-Ure

Morning

I wake up in the morning - alarm clocks tells me
I don't want to get up but the daylight taunts me.
The duvet is cosy but the smell of toast is calling.
'Oh for goodness sake, Sister, stop that opera
singing first thing in the morning!'

Dan Connor (10)
Skelton Newby Hall CE Primary School, Skelton-on-Ure

Going To York Dungeons

One day a girl named Judy wanted to go to York Dungeons but Judy's mum and dad said, 'No, not this week, maybe in three or four weeks.'

'But please!'

'Go to bed.'

Judy went to bed.

'Please!'

'Yes,' said Mum, 'we are going in a minute.'

James Wills (9)

Skelton Newby Hall CE Primary School, Skelton-on-Ure

The Dark Figure At The Door

Sitting on the sofa, I was alone at home. Mum and Dad took my brother to see a film. Suddenly the doorbell rang. I got up and peeped through the mailbox. I saw a dark figure. I helplessly hid my eyes; it was my dad, he'd forgotten his wallet.

Emily Harriman (9)
Swinefleet Primary School, Swinefleet

Look Out!

I fell out of my bed. I felt something moving under my bed. It pulled me under. Slime oozed all over me. It bit me and threw me back out. It was my cheeky little brother, Lukey the vampire! He'd been hunting again.

Adam Brown (8)
Swinefleet Primary School, Swinefleet

The Day The Biscuit Tin Went Missing

As I sneaked into the kitchen, I looked all around me, all was silent. I tiptoed to the cupboard and swung open the door. To my surprise, I found a Martian jumping out of the window with my biscuit tin. I was screaming as the Martian ran away. *Crumbs!*

Harvey Blyth (9)

Swinefleet Primary School, Swinefleet

The Weird Christmas

On a frosty winter's evening, around midnight,
I heard screaming. Something yelled, 'Merry
Christmas blub.' I was very confused. I heard
banging getting louder and louder which meant
something was getting closer to me.
Suddenly I saw my fish on stilts with a
microphone.
It was the weirdest night ever!

Olivia Farrar (10)
Swinefleet Primary School, Swinefleet

The Flying Fish

Whilst fishing with my cousin, we found a flying fish. But it was green with red eyes, purple wings and vampire teeth. It jumped out of the water and thousands more appeared and jumped out as well. My cousin was bitten by one. I ran for my life ...

Oliver Burrows (10)
Swinefleet Primary School, Swinefleet

The Two Dogs

In an enormous cave there were two dogs called Weeny and Tiny but they didn't know that there was a dragon who blew fire. Suddenly Tiny and Weeny smelt the fire so they ran for their lives but Weeny fell over, so Tiny risked her life for her best friend.

Connor Davy (9)
Swinefleet Primary School, Swinefleet

Boggle Green 2

The human-like creature rose from its green slimy brew. As it climbed out, its slimy surface turned rubbery and began to bounce. With its arms gesticulating and mouth gurgling, it bounced towards me like a tennis ball. The monstrous slime had turned out to be a cute, bouncy ball!

Georgia Cowling (11)
Swinefleet Primary School, Swinefleet

The Dream That Might Have Happened

On Christmas Eve, I was in bed. I heard a noise. *Was it a burglar?* I went down to investigate. My heart was racing. Suddenly I saw Santa. I didn't know what to do. I ran upstairs.
Suddenly I woke up - it was just a dream, *or was it?*

Georgia Harriman (10)
Swinefleet Primary School, Swinefleet

The Return Of My Finger

As I climbed Mount Everest, a rock fell on
my finger and broke it off. I staggered home,
desperate to find a bandage. I found a bandage
and wrapped it round rapidly but to my surprise,
something crawled from the window and
dropped into my hand. It was my finger!

Ethan Birbeck (10)
Swinefleet Primary School, Swinefleet

The Day A Plutonian Came For A Visit

I can remember it like it was yesterday! It happened about midnight. I was having another restless night. Suddenly bright lights were flashing outside my bedroom window. Then, *puff!* A weird alien arrived in my room. He wrote, 'Me from Pluto,' on my blackboard. Then, *puff!* He was gone!

David McKone (10)
Swinefleet Primary School, Swinefleet

Creepy Houses

I step into my house, nobody's there. I go into my kitchen, there's a strange man. I don't know him! I run out of my house to my friend's house. There is nobody there. I go into her bedroom, there is a strange man standing there, I don't know him!

Jennifer Austwick (9)
Swinefleet Primary School, Swinefleet

The Lake Nose Monster

As Matthew walked alone by the lake, he thought he spotted a fish. However, he soon realised it was a slimy-nosed monster, crawling out towards him. Matthew screamed his head off and ran towards the woods at full speed. The monster pushed through the woods and Matthew sprinted away.

George Cooper (9)
Swinefleet Primary School, Swinefleet

Untitled

I could see the sea but the question was, what lurked under there? I saw the most peculiar thing in the water, dived in to explore … I thought I was dreaming but I wasn't! I saw a gigantic whale, shark and lantern fish combined in one. Suddenly it went dark …

Natasha Faxon (10)
Swinefleet Primary School, Swinefleet

The Mystery At School

Friday was a regular day but Saturday, the streets were empty. Monday at school, oddly no one was there. I noticed scratches on the wall, blood dripping down the door. I took a peek. There lay a beast feasting on my head teacher. It saw me so I was doomed ...

Chloe Hansard (9)
Swinefleet Primary School, Swinefleet

The Big Drop

The wind took my breath away, my hair felt like
it was blowing off my head. Would I survive such
a big drop? I let out a big scream. *'Argh!'* The end
was nearer, I could see.
Phew! I'd made it. That was such a cool ride.

Kean Noon (9)
Swinefleet Primary School, Swinefleet

The Santa Invasion

I went to a Christmas car boot sale on Sunday
and bought a Christmas tree, a model reindeer, a
great Santa suit and a sleigh.
At home later, all the lights were off, it was really
dark. There was a rapping at the door.
It was Santa in his vest!

Louis Brown (8)
Swinefleet Primary School, Swinefleet

Scared

The house was dark, I was so scared. I saw a shadow on the wall, it looked like a two-headed monster. I saw it creep behind my back, it tapped me on my shoulder. *'Boo!'* said Amy-Jess.

Niamh Dowson (8)
Swinefleet Primary School, Swinefleet

The Death

I awoke in darkness that enclosed me. I lay on a damp surface that was seeping through my clothes. A piercing scream echoed in the blackening night. I ran! As I sprinted, the tree's arms grabbed me.
I saw her! A werewolf was towering above. Too late … Death had arrived!

Molly Mennie (11)
Thorne Green Top Primary School, Thorne

Almost Alien Encounter

The bright light blinded me like the beam from a torch. It grew closer. Closer still. I could not move. Suddenly it ferociously threw itself at me, viciously. An alien from space was duelling with me! Well not quite an alien. More like my cousin. 'I didn't mean to ...'

Morgan Wardle (11)
Thorne Green Top Primary School, Thorne

Patch Goes For A Walk

Patch went for a walk. What was the best bit? Fresh air blowing his fur as he chased his spotty ball? His friend Gypsy playing with him? Playing in puddles? Chasing raindrops as they fell from the sky? *No!* His favourite part was curling by the fire afterwards! Silly Patch!

Holly Brennan (11)
Tranmoor Primary School, Armthorpe

A Strange Figure

It was midnight, all was quiet. Suddenly Molly woke with a start. *What was that?* Creeping downstairs, cautiously peeping round the corner, a large dumpy figure was rummaging in a large sack next to the Christmas tree. His large feet carefully padded across the old floor! It was Santa!

Jade Duffield (11)
Tranmoor Primary School, Armthorpe

The Day The World Ended!

It all started on April 5th 2082. Kimberley and Jake were bunking off school. *Bang!* There was an unexplained thud! Suddenly there was a scream. They ran to the abandoned alley! There was a man lying with bullets through his chest! He then stood up and just walked away!

Beth Hale (13)
Tranmoor Primary School, Armthorpe

The Box In The Storm

I watched my reflection being chopped about in the sea. The wind howled, rain lashed down on the beach. Suddenly the world turned white through lightning. All was still! I turned to run. Then I saw a big box appear before me. But nobody was there ... or was there?

Katie May (11)
Wigginton Primary School, Wigginton

Mirror, Mirror

'Mirror, mirror on the wall. Who is the fairest one of all?'
The mirror replied, 'For it is Snow White. Ruby red lips and hair black as night. Her skin pale as snow and she always wears a big red bow.'

Megan Wetten (11)
Wigginton Primary School, Wigginton

The Snowy Mountain

Climbing up the biggest snowy mountain I've ever seen, I heard a faint howl. Racing elegantly to the top, my heart was beating as fast as a cheetah could run. Then, up on the top, I saw a soft golden puppy. I took it home.

Aimée Swan (10)
Wigginton Primary School, Wigginton

Who's There?

The corridor was long. Very long. I strolled along it, my head held high, but inside I was nervous, my stomach doing somersaults. Then I saw a tall, slim figure in the distance reaching out an arm. Then the lights flickered and all of a sudden they turned on.

Anna Bertram (10)

Wigginton Primary School, Wigginton

The Spook's Medicine!

I drank another sip of the vile liquid, my eyes started to turn. My ears started to bleed, I took another sip of the medicine, there, I was resting in peace.

'Wakey, wakey! Come downstairs and take this medicine, it makes you feel a whole lot better!'

'Nnnooo!'

Katie Wilson (10)

Wigginton Primary School, Wigginton

It Was ...

Like a giant mourning, the sound was horrific.
Eee-ooo-eee-ooo! I awoke. Time check - 2.07am.
Creeping from my tent, I listened anxiously. The
sea glimmered like diamonds before me.
Eee-ooo-eee-ooo! What is it? It's so weird.
As I tiptoed towards the cliff edge, a strong hand
gripped my shoulder! It was ...

Amy Berry (10)
Wigginton Primary School, Wigginton

Seeing Things At The Beach

One sunny day, I decided to go to the beach. A girl sat with me. She said her name was Amber. We enjoyed an ice cream together. At home time she said she had loved my company. Her image became fuzzy then she disappeared.
Was Amber real or a ghost?

Ellie Roberts (10)
Wigginton Primary School, Wigginton

A Disloyal Friend

Inspector Horner paced up and down, thinking. *Suspect one was in the right place at the right time but suspect two* … his phone rang. He answered it and said, 'I've got her laptop.' Aha. Criminal two was the criminal after all. Long weeks evidence-finding; it was my disloyal friend!

Alice Robinson (10)
Wigginton Primary School, Wigginton

It

I could feel something coming up behind me …
something with bloodshot eyes and razor-sharp
teeth; bloodstained fur. Chasing me. Closer …
closer. Chasing me through the windmill, my
heartbeat the same pace as the giant fans.
I'd lost it for now. You must agree,
I'd been through the mill!

Kieran Yews (11)
Wigginton Primary School, Wigginton

The Miserable Criminal

The rain lashed down and her head looked up. The inspector saw the suspect's tears long before he saw her face. For she may be the one who took the money. In her plea for freedom, he couldn't look at her face, for she was the thief. The miserable criminal.

Molly Horner (10)
Wigginton Primary School, Wigginton

Talking Potatoes

'When did you get eaten?' asked Wedge.
'Last week!' replied Chip.
'Don't ask me how I'm doing or when I got eaten,
you are my best potato chip.
Now you leave me out on this special day in my
life!' Jacket interrupted.
'Why?' they asked.
'Because it's my *birthday!*'

Ellie Stewart (10)
Wigginton Primary School, Wigginton

A Night After School

All was quiet in a dark house when Kelly got home. Nobody was in sight. A light flicked in the living room. It came on again but stayed on.
'*Booo!*' It was a birthday surprise!
'Happy birthday, Kelly!' said everyone. 'Here are your presents Kelly.'

Ryan Brown (10)
Wigginton Primary School, Wigginton

How The Earth Came To Be ...

As two pizzas hurtled through the galaxy, one
topped with chilli and ice cream, the other with
baked beans and egg, no one could see the
amazing phenomenon that was about to occur.
The four elements collided to make our Earth the
biggest calzone in the universe ever!

Alice Wilson (11)
Wigginton Primary School, Wigginton

The Joker Called Isabel

Once upon a time there was a jolly, jumpy joker called Isabel. She always wore a pink top, black leggings, pink boots. She rode a horse called Emma.

Next door, on the farm, lived a wolf. The wolf attacked the horse and killed it.

Isabel Marks cried for two days.

Isabel Marks (10)

Windmill Hill Primary School, Chapeltown

The Boy, Tom, Looking For Some Wool

On a large, smelly farm, local boy Tom asked for some jet-black wool. Farmer Jack said he could have some but only if he took some to the master, John, and some to the dame, Holly. Then Tom took his black wool down the winding, narrow lane.

Josh Ronson (7)
Windmill Hill Primary School, Chapeltown

Humpty Dumpty Sat On A Loo

Humpty Dumpty had a poo, then he fell down the smelly, rotten loo. Then the stupid soldiers came to help him. They broke his leg, broke his arm and boiled him. Then he was a boiled, dirty, rotten egg.
Then the loo was flushed.

Kai Bates (10)
Windmill Hill Primary School, Chapeltown

Tom And Bill

Tom and Bill went up the hill to fetch a pail of
clean water. Tom fell down and broke his gold,
metal crown and Bill came tumbling after, down
the steep grassy hill.
Suddenly Tom lost his shirt and shouted out loud,
'It was my new shirt, it's ruined forever!'

Bethany Hindley (9)
Windmill Hill Primary School, Chapeltown

The Magic Book

I peered through a door and saw a very peculiar book. As I went to pick it up, there was a beam of light. A woman stood in front of me. I tried to run away but it was too late.
The book opened and I was sucked inside forever ...

Charlotte Hayhoe (9)
Worsbrough Common Primary School, Barnsley

Phew!

Tension built up as the vast boat hit the immense
iceberg. Rose screamed in horror as the boat
tilted. They clung on, petrified, unsure whether it
was a life or death situation!
Splash! A huge amount of people poured into
the water.
Phew! They were only at the cinema!

Regan Birtles (10)
Worsbrough Common Primary School, Barnsley

Laura And The Door

Laura walked down a long corridor. As she strolled, she noticed a vast door. Its big, cold padlock stiff, she was frozen to the spot. She put her small, shivering hands on it and it opened with a small creak then she entered …
The vast, cold freezer made her shiver.

Sapphire Liversidge (10)
Worsbrough Common Primary School, Barnsley

Untitled

The three blind mice were skipping round Miss
Polly's kitchen when suddenly there came an
immense bang! The grand old Duke of York
marched his soldiers down the hill to see what all
the commotion was about.
Humpty's wall had been demolished! The doctor
sent him to bed really early!

Chloe Morley (10)
Worsbrough Common Primary School, Barnsley

Weirdly Day

This was an unusual planet. Sort of alien. The strange man had two eyes, brightly coloured skin. Out in the space garden, was Dad, staring at himself. He heard a loud noise. Dad was scared. It was on his grass. He crept to it.
Phew! It was only his lawnmower.

Caitlin Reynolds (10)

Worsbrough Common Primary School, Barnsley

Harry Potter Falls In Love

One day in the hall, Harry was banging on the secret passage to get into the potion club. He ran. In one minute, he was in love with the most beautiful girl in the whole school and then, *kiss!* He fell in love forever.

Emma Dawber (11)
Worsbrough Common Primary School, Barnsley

Information

We hope you have enjoyed reading this book - and that you will continue to enjoy it in the coming years.

If you like reading and writing, drop us a line or give us a call and we'll send you a free information pack. Alternatively visit our website at www.youngwriters.co.uk

Write to:
Young Writers Information,
Remus House,
Coltsfoot Drive,
Peterborough,
PE2 9JX

Tel: (01733) 890066
Email: youngwriters@forwardpress.co.uk